Special Message

_____
_____
_____
_____
_____

With Love, _____

Stick your favorite
picture here

Amora

is surrounded with so much love.
You may even think it comes from above.

Amora

You are loved by the sky and the sun.

You deserve happiness and to have so much fun.

Amora

You are loved by the trees and the leaves that fall.

You are loved by everyone and all.

Amora

You are loved by the wind and the breeze.
You deserve the best hugging squeeze.

Amora

You are loved by the birds that tweet.

All because you are so gentle and sweet.

Amora

You are loved by the flowers
in the ground.
There is so much love all around.

Amora

You are loved by the moon and night.
You shine like the stars with the brightest light.

Amora

You are loved with your beautiful heart.

You are beautiful, amazing, and oh so smart.

Amora

You are love from your head to your toes.

You are loved by your family so close.

Merry Christmas.
Love, Grandma

Amora

You will be loved for the rest of your days.
You will be loved forever and always.

The end